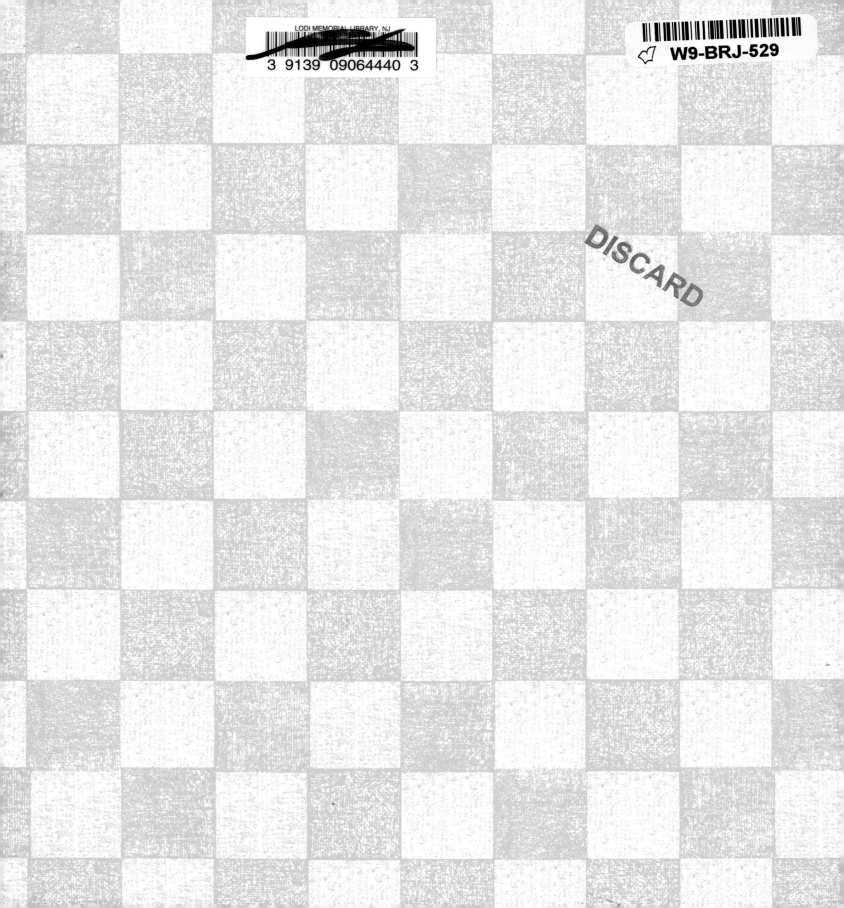

A GIFT FROM ABUELA

Cecilia Ruiz

CANDLEWICK PRESS

Abuela would never forget the day Niña was born.
It was an unusual day in Mexico City. On this day,
the sky was clear and the streets were still.

Abuela's heart overflowed with tenderness the moment she held Niña for the first time. Though Niña might not remember it, she felt cozy and loved in Abuela's arms.

Niña and Abuela spent a lot of time together.
They liked making up silly songs.

They loved spinning around
until they both felt dizzy.

Abuela liked teaching Niña how
to make *papel picado* banners.

And Niña loved making
Abuela laugh.

But their favorite thing of all was a much simpler one. Every Sunday, they would sit quietly in the park, eat *pan dulce*, and watch the people pass by.

PAN DULCE
10 PESOS

One day, Abuela had an idea. She would save twenty pesos every week until she had enough money to buy Niña a very special gift.

Maybe a bike she could ride to school.

Maybe a puppy she could play with.

Or maybe Abuela could take Niña to see the ocean for the first time.

And that's just what Abuela did. Every Friday after work, she would put a few pesos away in her secret spot.

Time passed. Niña got older. Abuela got older, too.
And life got harder in Mexico.

ESCUELA

Things just kept getting more expensive.
People were hungry and upset.

Things got difficult for Abuela, too.
One week, she had no extra pesos
to put away in her secret spot.

Then the government changed the money.
People had to turn in their old bills for
nuevos pesos. The old bills became worthless.

Other things changed, too. Niña would play with her friends after school and didn't go to see Abuela as much.

Abuela had to work twice as much and was always tired.
It's not that they didn't love each other anymore.
Sometimes life just gets in the way.

One day, Niña realized it had been a long time since she had seen Abuela, so she went for a visit.

When she arrived, Abuela was not there.
The house looked sad and dusty.

I know, thought Niña. *I'll surprise her*.

Everything will be nice and clean by the time
she gets back, she thought.

Then Niña noticed a jar tucked away. It was full of money—
old money. *Oh no*, thought Niña. *It's all worthless.*

When Abuela returned and saw Niña, her heart overflowed with tenderness.

"Niña!" said Abuela. "I'm so glad to see you! And look at my kitchen!"

"I wanted to do something nice for you," said Niña.
"Look what I found."

"I wanted to buy you a very special gift," Abuela explained sadly. "But I must have forgotten where I kept my savings. And now the money is worthless."

"It's okay," said Niña. "I have an idea."

With the old bills, Niña and Abuela made the
most beautiful *papel picado* banners.

That Sunday, Abuela and Niña went to the park, ate *pan dulce*, and watched the people pass by.

It was still their favorite thing to do.

To my loving parents

First edition 2018

Library of Congress Catalog Card Number pending
ISBN 978-0-7636-9267-4

18 19 20 21 22 23 CCP 10 9 8 7 6 5 4 3 2 1

Printed in Shenzhen, Guangdong, China

This book was typeset in ITC Novarese.
The illustrations were done in mixed media.

Candlewick Press
99 Dover Street
Somerville, Massachusetts 02144

visit us at www.candlewick.com